PRAISE FOR
The Little Girl Who Grew Up to Be Governor

"This beautiful story of one of the first woman governors delights, enchants, teaches, and inspires. For girls, it points to a path of self-discovery, leadership, and service. For us older ones, it evokes an earlier time of political life guided by purpose and caring, thus pointing us to a path of service inspired by our predecessors." —Margaret J. Wheatley, author of multiple books on leadership, community, and service

"Plainly and beautifully written, Frances Smith Strickland's poignant book inspires young people and especially young women to step forward as leaders now and prepare to be leaders when they are adults. She uses the power of engaging storytelling that every child loves, to bring the lessons of what it means to lead and be a leader right into the heart and mind of the reader. It's a great book for children. Come to think of it, by portraying leaders at their very best, it's a book that today's adult leaders would do well to be reading, too." —Andy Hargreaves, Professor Emeritus, Boston College

"This book is a powerful reminder that there is a nobility to public service and political life. As declared in the book: 'The government is a system of people working together to make rules and laws about how to live well together.' This is also a narrative about leadership, raising and educating our children. Plus the fact that women have it within them, perhaps uniquely, to create a future of working together. Even though it is a slice of history, it speaks to tomorrow—something badly needed at this moment in time." —Peter Block, author and citizen of Cincinnati, Ohio

"By the time I finished chapter one, I was enthralled! I read the whole thing in one sitting. It's beautiful! It really moved me. The description of what both political parties should be is wonderful. This may be a children's book, but it is 'right on' for people of all ages!" —Ian Mitroff, Senior Research Affiliate, UC Berkeley

"What a wonderful idea for a children's book! Just loved it."
—Douglas Brinkley, Professor of History at Rice University

"We found *The Little Girl Who Grew Up to Be Governor* totally engaging and charming. Our nine-year-old granddaughter is super excited about this book! And, the idea of keeper stories will lead readers to think about memories from their own lives. The manner of explaining how the political system works was impressive. And, we loved 'how sweet it is' that more women are being elected!" —Governor Jay Inslee & First Lady Trudi Inslee, Washington state

"I give *The Little Girl Who Grew Up to Be Governor* a ringing endorsement! We need more female leadership in all sectors, especially in our political system. Teaching girls about the possibilities in the formative years is a start to helping them Dream it, See it and Believe it! And my ultimate hope is that the first female President of the United States will have been a Girl Scout!" —Tammy Wharton, Girl Scouts of Ohio's Heartland Council President & CEO

"What Dr. Smith Strickland says is very reasonable, and certainly not controversial. Of course, we all show some interests when we are young that are not carried forth, and many also discover their passions and strengths later in life. Best wishes." —Howard Gardner, Hobbs Research Professor of Cognition and Education, Harvard

"I imagined that I was reading it to my great grand five-year-old. Even at five, she would have been caught by the early stories. The images of the farm, the characters, and the animals are wonderful. The stories tell the lessons. The illustrations are wonderful and, of course, it is so timely." —Mary Lazarus, community leader

"Our family loved this book! By sharing stories from Martha Layne's childhood, Dr. Smith Strickland charms young readers who find themselves rooting for their new friend as she learns to be a leader. The book gently balances the biographical tale of Martha while also teaching perseverance, the nobility of public service, and learning from mistakes with a touch of humor. Martha is a real Tom Sawyer, but this American girl grew up to be governor." —Janetta King & John Stephan, Silas age 7, Sylvia age 6

"I think the author has done an amazing job seamlessly including a more modern look at issues that affect kids these days. From the preface introducing the qualities of leadership all the way to Martha Layne's career as governor and public servant, the words pop off the page and she comes to life. The pacing is good and the flow creates interest in her adventures and in her life. I loved the illustrations, too. Kids can interact on so many levels with this writing." —Eva O'Mara, elementary school principal

"Thanks for sharing this cute little book. Each chapter opened and closed very nicely with a moral to the story. Clever and meaningful to young readers. I especially like the bipartisan explanation of our two-party system and the necessity of having both to keep our government in balance. The pictures were well placed and well done." —Tauwanta Corns, school administrator

"This book is VERY good! I liked the simple wording and balanced interpretation of the differences between Democrats and Republicans. It is truly bipartisan for kids in the way it stresses that both parties are equally important. The way it all hangs together is AMAZING!" —Becky Denham, Oregon physician

"*The Little Girl Who Grew Up to Be Governor* follows the path of ordinary events in a young girl's life as they resolve themselves into a lifetime of extraordinary achievements. Leadership is a primary theme, but the book also tells a story of childhood nurturing, risk-taking, failure, and experimentation. As the story progresses, there is a poignancy in the rich descriptions of growing up in a different time and in a place that probably no longer exists. It is the sweetness of these details that make the book likely to appeal not only to children but to adult readers as well."
—Linda Fenner, former school superintendent

"I LOVE this book! My Master's is in Children's Literature, so I've read lots of books for kids during my personal and professional life. I think this book about Martha Layne Collins is both informative and heartwarming. What fun to read! Now I want to learn more about her." —Jeanne Melvin, second and third-grade teacher

"All of us hope our children successfully apply the valuable lessons in their adult life that they've learned while growing up. *The Little Girl Who Grew Up to Be Governor* shows how successful Martha Layne Collins was at doing just that. Lessons of courage, helpfulness, kindness, independence, and perseverance are just some of them. This book sets good examples for all of our children no matter what they may choose to do in life."
—Alta Beasley, farmer

"I love the way the author has taken a prominent woman's life and looked back into her earliest years to examine the way she was formed. Our lived experiences end up being so foundational to who we become, even when we layer on education and vocation. Bravo for creating such a lovely story of the young woman who would become governor." —Shiloh Todorov, Matriots

"From the very first page, I found the author's writing style to be both current and approachable. Respecting her young readers, Dr. Smith Strickland never speaks down to them, even when dealing with difficult topics. ... Chapter after chapter presents specific examples of leadership that kids will grab onto and parents and teachers will use to enhance the many lessons that this book instills. A fine book when it was first published the first time and a masterful rewrite for today's world, one that is very much in need of personal exemplars of informed, caring leadership."
—Dr. James R. Delisle, professor, teacher, and speaker on behalf of gifted children

"We read this book and then discussed it. Not only did we enjoy reading it, we like the way each chapter lends itself to great discussions that many of the students can relate to: being brave, solving a problem, making plans, volunteering, being helpful, needing help, fairness, and sharing. A very fun teaching tool for elementary school children." —Angie Smith and Sherri Prose, second-grade teachers

"As the father of a daughter who is an only child, I was interested in any nuggets this appealing story of a Kentucky farm girl's journey into adulthood might provide readers. Dr. Smith Strickland's portrayal of Martha Layne Hall, a young girl who applied childhood learnings into life lessons that demonstrated how caring and responsibility formed her later political leadership and personal character, is a compelling narrative. This portrait of Governor Martha Layne Collins, Kentucky's only woman to serve in that office, provides a model for how easily character education can be delivered through appealing, authentic literature that serves as a vehicle to teach and inspire young readers and listeners." —Denis Smith, educator

"In *The Little Girl Who Grew Up to Be Governor*, Martha Layne Collins comes to life in vivid and highly relatable stories of her childhood. The author, Dr. Frances Smith Strickland, does a brilliant job of connecting those stories to important points about leadership and the qualities that make a person a good leader. The book also offers a meaningful framework—written in simple terms — for children and their parents to think about government, the political process, and the role of the major political parties. The book is both inspiring and a delight to read." —Peggy Cordray, professor, Capital University Law School

"I just finished reading *The Little Girl Who Grew Up to Be Governor* and loved it! I especially liked the way the (ideal) political process is explained in language kids will understand, that politicians have important jobs, such as to 'make sure there are schools' for all the kids. Or, the roles of the two political parties—one to come up with new ideas for solving societal problems, and the other to make sure those ideas are practical and will work. As one who taught history to seventh graders, I wish I'd had these insights at the time. This book should be read by every teacher-to-be. And every parent." —Jack Burgess, educator

"Former Ohio First Lady Frances Smith Strickland, Ph.D., has written *The Little Girl Who Grew Up to Be Governor* such that small children can understand the words of the adventures of Martha Layne Collins, who became the first woman governor of Kentucky. This is an excellent book for teachers to read to elementary students, and for schools to have available in their libraries. Compassion and deep understanding guide even her most painful experiences. Every adventure reinforces societal values that bring people together while sharing how government functions to help us have better lives, and what we can all do toward that end. A delightfully empowering book. And I learned a new word—bumfuzzle!" —Kathleen Burgess, writer

"I found this book an easy read that held my attention quite well. In teaching young children, I found they were ever so curious about real-life happenings. These down-to-earth examples showed how an ordinary little girl had goals and ideas and in her own way, was driven to carry them out. These traits opened up the door to her future success. Using this book as a teaching tool makes these lessons real—even for those in early childhood." —Edna Isaacs, Georgia teacher

"*The Little Girl Who Grew Up to Be Governor* is a wonderful story of possibilities and purpose. It tells the inspiring story of Kentucky's first woman governor in a way that takes us back to all the good things we experienced growing up. Children, as well as leaders at all levels of government, would do well to read and reflect upon the qualities of leadership recounted in these pages." —Mark Stewart, social studies teacher

"I read this little book two times—not because it was a difficult read but because it was so enjoyable. It contained so many life lessons! Things young children (and some adults) have never thought about or were never taught. Like how choosing to be a politician as a career is good—if you can imagine! A lot was packed into this little book, and I could go on and on. But I especially liked the story about how just the smallest of gestures to another person can have a meaningful impact on both of our lives. It is perfect for where society is today." —Jenny Conrad, businesswoman

"Revised and refreshed... These 'Keeper' Stories fill the pages of this delightful account of Martha Lane Collins's life and her journey to becoming Kentucky's first female governor. This compilation of heartwarming adventures spanning from her childhood to her retirement transport the reader back to a simpler time when respect, hard work, and helping others were not only taught but practiced. This book would be an excellent tool in teaching children to see the greater good in politics and to help them understand the process. Dr. Frances Smith Strickland does a superb job taking a very informative, educational, and non-partisan approach while sharing a glimpse of an amazing lady. This book definitely has my VOTE!" —Kimberly Brushart Byrd, elementary school teacher

"All through reading *The Little Girl Who Grew Up to Be Governor*, I kept thinking, 'Boy, is this relevant and needed for today's politicians and leaders! They need to be reminded of the deepest calling for such life works! I'm glad it's back in the hands of today's children!' Dr. Frances Strickland tells interesting, very accessible stories from the childhood of Kentucky's first woman Governor, Martha Layne Collins, and explains how the lessons from early experiences help shape the important qualities for those who lead and govern—qualities such as courage despite fear, problem-solving and willingness to listen and learn. Today's leaders as well as today's children can learn a lot from Dr. Smith Strickland's excellent book!" —Mimi Brodsky Chenfeld, author

"This book is full of universal values that transcend cultures and boundaries. Themes include dreaming and following those dreams; loving and caring for self, family, and others; being courageous in the face of difficulties; being curious and learning from one's mistakes; engaging with others and building a helping community to make lives better; and always being the best you you can be. This book provides time-honored examples for people of all ages." —Harold and Jean Bussell, grandparents

"This inspiring little book ought to be a primer for any college level course on women in politics. Delightfully plain and simple, it is still deeply thought provoking with much to consider. Using the experiences of Governor Collins of Kentucky, Dr. Smith Strickland describes political party orientation in unbiased and easily understandable terms—including running for political office, being elected, and navigating the legislative process. It becomes clear that leadership and social responsibility are skills to be taught and learned just like math or science and, as such, deserve our deliberate attention both at home and in school and in all the communities in which we interact. We highly recommend this book as bedtime stories for little people—boys and girls alike—and for more serious consideration by the rest of us." —Becky & Craig Strafford, physicians

"Dr. Smith Strickland's book *The Little Girl Who Grew Up to Be Governor*, Second Edition is full of fun and educational stories, painting a picture of how a young girl in a small town in Kentucky grew up to be a woman whose leadership was decades before its time. The anecdotes Dr. Smith Strickland shares from Martha Layne Collins' childhood, with otherworldly adventure and familiar lessons for children today, demonstrate why the things kids do — their curiosities, what they find fun, the adventures they go on — are all important influences on whom they will be as adults. Martha Layne's example encourages children to trust their instincts while empowering them to believe that the things that pull them today are not something they should one day grow out of, but in fact are crucial building blocks to who they will become. In a world full of things that we should do, Dr. Smith Strickland's book is a lesson in why doing what we want to do, and being exactly who we are, will lead to making the greatest impact on the world. As a dancer would say, bravo!" —Abby Corrigan, professional dancer

"Martha Layne Collins's uplifting and inspiring story humanizes the American political process for children learning about our precious democracy for the first time. In these times of political strife and social stress, this charming book provides much-needed lessons in genuine leadership, generosity, and the true meaning of service to the greater good." —Julie Henahan, retired arts administrator

"We need some good inspiring books like this for old people to read to young people." —Tom O'Grady, Director, Athens County Historical Society and Museum

"*The Little Girl Who Grew Up to Be Governor* melts away many of the negative stereotypes of public service and restores it to its rightful place. A lighthearted, but serious read that anyone would deem fascinating and inspiring, this fresh embodiment of Dr. Smith Strickland's original work fits, perfectly, the times in which we now live. It is a reminder that learning is a lifelong endeavor, and our failures are very often an important part of our successes." —Joan Dearth, educator

"Frances Smith Strickland's revised second edition of *The Little Girl Who Grew Up to Be Governor* is a delightful read! Young readers, especially girls, will be inspired by the easy and relatable growing up stories of real life Martha Layne Collins who indeed did grow up to become Governor of Kentucky. Along with the stories are the conversation starters about lessons that can be learned in leadership and life from our ordinary experiences, challenges, and dreams. I'd encourage anyone to read this chapter book with children and go with where it takes them." —Jim Mahoney, retired school superintendent

"Many teachable moments can be shared while reading this to elementary-age students. The reader comes away knowing what good government should do...it's important to find ways to help that don't break the rules! Personal sharing, family sharing, public sharing...so many things to expand upon and give children the inspiration to pursue their goals. *The Little Girl Who Grew Up to Be Governor* is definitely a keeper."
—Carmella Gentile, retired teacher

The Little Girl Who Grew Up to Be Governor

Leadership Lessons and Stories
From the Life of Martha Layne Collins

Second Edition

Written by Frances Smith Strickland, Ph.D.
Illustrated by Pip Pullen

Copyright © 1991; Second Edition, 2021 Frances Smith Strickland

All rights reserved.

No portion of this book may be reproduced, translated, stored in a retrieval system, or transmitted in any form or by any means, electronic, mechanical, photocopying, microfilming, recording, or otherwise without written permission from the publisher.

Printed in the United States of America.
Published by The Compassionate Mind Collaborative (cmcollab.com)

ISBN: 978-1-7372006-0-4 (Paperback)
ISBN: 978-1-7372006-1-1 (Ebook)
Library of Congress Control Number: 202191257020219125702021912570

Illustrated by Pip Pullen
Edited by Heather Doyle Fraser
Designed by Danielle Baird
Proofed by Jesse Sussman

Dream dreams, study hard, work hard and you can grow up to be anything you want to be! Always, be the best that you can be!!!

Martha Layne Collins
Governor of Kentucky
1983-1987

Teaching and Learning Guides
for Educators and Parents

Are you an elementary school educator who would like to learn more about how to use this book in your classroom?

Are you a parent who would like to have some discussion questions to use with your young reader as you read this book together?

If you answered yes to either of these questions, check out the teaching and learning guides for *The Little Girl Who Grew Up to Be Governor: Leadership Lessons and Stories From the Life of Martha Layne Collins,* Second Edition by Frances Smith Strickland, Ph.D.

Available Fall 2021 on the website for the book at **www.kidsareleaders.org.**

Contents

Preface 15

Chapter 1   Making People Happy. 21

Part I   **The Little Girl...**

Chapter 2   Martha Layne Discovers People 29

Chapter 3   The First Journey. 33

Chapter 4   Scared but Hanging In 39

Chapter 5   There *Has to Be* a Way. 45

Chapter 6   Looking Ahead 51

Chapter 7   The Helper Needs Help. 57

Chapter 8   Understanding Changes 63

Chapter 9   Making Things Better 69

Chapter 10   The Hard Worker 75

Chapter 11   "I Can Do That!" 79

Chapter 12   The Leader 85

Part II   **...Who Grew Up...**

Chapter 13   Martha Layne Collins. 93

Chapter 14   The Politician. 99

Part III ...To Be Governor

Chapter 15 Governor of Kentucky 113

Chapter 16 Keeping Her Promise 123

Part IV Words from Governor Collins

Chapter 17 Keepers. 133

Appendix

Female Governors Elected In Their Own Right 141

Female Governors Under Special Circumstances . . 145

About the Author 147

Acknowledgments 151

Preface

You might think that the things you do when you are little are not anything special. But they are—very special. They might just give you a clue as to what you are going to be or do when you grow up.

No matter how old you are, your parents and grandparents will always enjoy watching the things you do. They pay the most attention to the things you decide to do on your own—how you "entertain" yourself. Your play shows them what you are interested in and what you want to learn more about.

There are at least three ways that you show others what you like to do and what you want to learn more about. The first way is what you do when you are up and moving around. Some children are always dancing even when no music is playing. Others want to go outside and kick a soccer ball or throw a baseball, or dribble and shoot a basketball, maybe even climb on something like a climbing wall. If you keep practicing and learn more and more, let's say about dancing, you just might grow up to be a dancer. If a particular sport excites you and draws you in, you may grow up to be an athlete.

The second way is how you show your feelings. It's always good to be happy, but sometimes you feel scared, or mad, or sad. Most children use their words to say how they feel inside. But, some draw pictures, or use stories and songs, or act them out in plays. Many children who choose these ways to show their feelings grow up to be artists, musicians, actors, or writers.

The third way you tell parents about yourself is in how you use your toys and take care of your pets. For example, are you able to play with your toys without breaking them? If one breaks, do you try to fix it? You might not know it, but when engineers and architects were your age, they liked to fix and build things. If you have a pet, do you make sure it has food and water every day? Veterinarians grew up caring about all kinds of animals, especially those that were sick or hurt. Do you love saving the environment and learning how things grow? When scientists were your age, they loved exploring outside in nature.

This book is about a little girl who loved people and taking care of animals. She was forever dreaming up new ways to be with them and to make them happy. She learned that if you want to help a lot of people all at one time, you need others to join in. And when people work together, they usually need a leader to help everyone know what to do. So, she didn't grow up to be a doctor or nurse, or even a veterinarian. She grew up to be a leader.

You know many leaders. For instance, your teachers are leaders. Without them, you and your classmates would have a very hard time learning and playing together. Coaches in sports are leaders. Girl Scouts and Boy Scouts have troop leaders.

Martha Layne Collins grew up to be a special kind of leader. She became a political leader. It is important for you to know about political leaders because many of the things you care about need their help. Like, if you are worried about animals being mistreated, politicians make laws to protect them. When there is a dangerous virus threatening to make everyone sick, politicians make sure there are vaccines that keep your family safe. They help people hurt by floods or tornadoes find food and a place to live. And they make sure there are schools to teach children the many things they need to know and learn.

Martha Layne grew up to be a special political leader. She became the governor of Kentucky. That means she worked to help all of the people that lived in her state. These stories about her as a little girl and what she did as she was growing up gave clues that she might one day be a leader. As you read these stories, think about the things you like to do. If you love people as much as she did and are always looking for more and more ways to be helpful, maybe you, too, will grow up to be a governor. Or, just maybe, president.

Frances Smith Strickland, Ph.D.
Author

Chapter 1

Making People Happy

It was very early in the morning but eleven-year-old Martha Layne Hall only had to be called once. She had waited for this day with great anticipation. Leaping out of bed, she quickly changed into the clothes her mother laid out the night before. She was going on a new adventure.

Martha Layne was always ready for a new adventure, but this one was special. Her father, Everett Hall, was taking her to see the President of the United States, Mr. Harry Truman. It would mean missing a little part of the school day, but that was all right. President Truman was a very important person and important people didn't come to their town very often. Her teacher knew that seeing President Truman was an amazing once-in-a-lifetime opportunity!

President Truman was coming to Shelbyville, Kentucky on a "Whistle-Stop Tour." Martha Layne had never heard of a whistle-stop tour and asked her father what it was. He explained that President Truman was traveling across the United States on a train, stopping at each railroad station along the way. As the train pulls into the railroad station, the engineer blows the whistle. That's why it is called a whistle stop. People gather around the red caboose at the end of the train. It is like a stage with a railing where President Truman stands and makes a speech to everyone. Once he finishes, the train moves to the next town and he talks to the people there.

President Truman's train ride took thirty-one days and covered 31,000 miles of train tracks. He made 352 speeches to the three million people that gathered around his red caboose day after day. Many writers said this train trip is what made it possible for him to keep on being president.

This day in 1948, Martha Layne and her father made their way to the railroad station. A large group of people were already there. She had never before seen them so excited and happy. They were all dressed up—as if it was Sunday or some other very special day. Martha Layne took in everything going on around her as she and her father moved toward the caboose.

"I still can't believe it," she heard one woman say.

"I know," replied her friend. "We've never had a president come here before."

Just then, they heard the sound of the train whistle off in the distance.

Someone yelled, "He's coming! I hear the train!"

Suddenly, grown-ups crushed in on all sides of Martha Layne. The only way she could see anything was to stand on her tiptoes.

Mr. Hall saw what was happening. He knew she'd never be able to see President Truman with so many people standing in her way. With one quick sweep of his strong arms, she was sitting on his shoulders. He was a very tall man.

Now, she could see over everyone's head.

A few minutes more and the great iron machine rolled into sight—a proud, powerful giant. As its metal wheels ground to a halt, the screeching was so loud that Martha Layne had to cover her ears. Finally stopped, the monster hissed billows of steam into the fair October sky. It seemed to command: *"Look at me! I'm strong! I'm magnificent."* But the train, in all its glory, could not compete with President Truman.

Even before he stepped out on the platform, the people cheered and clapped wildly. Some put their fingers in the side of their mouths and blew out a piercing whistle. Others yelled his name. When President Truman finally appeared, the clapping got even louder. Eager hands reached up to him. Smiling, he leaned down from his perch and shook every hand he could reach.

Martha Layne watched it all from atop her father's shoulders. "How wonderful it must be," she thought, "to be able to make so many people feel good, just by coming to see them." Little did she know that thirty-five years later an even larger crowd would line the streets to see her.

Children would miss school. Some would sit on the shoulders of their fathers so they could see her as she passed by.

Friends would crane their necks and strain their eyes to see her. They would ask each other, "Where is she? When will she be here?"

Finally someone would shout, "Here she comes! See the red coat? She's up there on the coach. See her? She's sitting by the driver."

They were waiting for the first woman ever elected as governor of Kentucky.

What Martha Layne didn't know as she rode in on that carriage was how many of the things she did as a little girl prepared her for this historic day. From the time she was barely old enough to walk, she was always eager to learn new things. She worked very hard, and had the courage to try new things even when she was scared.

But, most of all—just like good leaders—she wanted to be helpful.

Part I
The Little Girl...

Chapter 2

Martha Layne Discovers People

Mary and Everett Hall should have known their daughter was going to have a lot of energy when she decided to come into the world in the middle of the night. Martha Layne Hall was born at three o'clock in the morning on December 7, 1936—and it was freezing outside.

Cars in those days didn't have good heaters and many of the roads were full of ruts and very bumpy. But the Halls didn't mind the frosty night or the jarring ten-mile drive from the small town of Bagdad, Kentucky to the nearest hospital in Shelbyville. They were ready for the birth of their only child.

When Mr. Hall heard he had a little girl, it suited him just fine. In fact, he was overjoyed. As for Mrs. Hall, she now had a little companion to talk to while she worked. She told Martha Layne all kinds of things. Of course, Martha Layne didn't hear much of it since she slept most of the time.

Bagdad, where Martha Layne lived with her parents, had only about 250 people. That meant if the whole town decided to go on a vacation together, they would all fit into one airplane.

Sunday was always a special time because those who went to church believed it was a day of rest and worship. They weren't supposed to work. For Martha Layne, it was the time she got to be with lots of people. Even more special, when church was over families often went to each other's homes and ate a big meal together.

Martha Layne spent a lot of time at church. Her first experience was in the Ladies Sunday School Class. Mrs. Hall started taking her to the class when she was just two months old. The women sat in a big circle and talked to each other. Martha Layne usually slept quietly in her mother's lap on a little puffy blue ruffled pillow. She seemed very content on that little pillow, that is, until the day she discovered children.

It all began one Sunday when a teacher named Sally talked Mrs. Hall into letting her take Martha Layne to her class of five-year-old boys and girls. When Sally walked into the room with Martha Layne, the children all crowded around. They were enchanted by their special little visitor. Sally told them if they were very quiet and listened closely to their Sunday school lesson, she would stop a little early and they could play with Martha Layne.

Of course, the children were very good and before long, five little faces were huddled over the cute little baby. They did everything they could think of to get her attention. One put his thumbs in his ears and wiggled his stubby fingers.

Another pushed on her stomach and said, "Hi, little baby!" This upset a little girl in the class. "Donnnn't!" She warned. "You might hurt her!" Most of the others just grinned and watched.

When Mrs. Hall came to get her little girl, she wondered what in the world was going on.

From that time on when she went to church, Martha Layne wiggled and squirmed on her little pillow. She wanted to be in the class with the children.

Martha Layne's love of people and interest in them continued all her life. It didn't matter if they were young, middle-age, or older. But it was important that people liked her, too. Good leaders know that the more people like each other, the more many wonderful things they can do together.

Chapter 3

The First Journey

Like most children who don't have brothers or sisters, Martha Layne spent a lot of time entertaining herself. Back in the 1930s and 1940s, children didn't have iPads or video games and their parents were too busy to play with them. Her favorite thing to do was to go outside, even by herself. Somehow, there was always more to do outdoors, especially in a small town like Bagdad.

One afternoon when Martha Layne was about three years old, she asked to play outside. Her mother said "yes." But first, Martha Layne had to put on a bonnet. Her skin was very fair. She could easily get a bad sunburn.

Mrs. Hall knew it was safe for Martha Layne to play in the yard alone because it was completely surrounded by a tall fence. There was a gate but it was much too difficult for a young child to open by herself. So, she was not worried that Martha Layne would wander off. Just the same, Mrs. Hall kept an eye on her through the kitchen window.

One particular day, Martha Layne must have run out of things to do because she decided to go visiting. She went to the gate, but it was fastened and wouldn't open. Just as Mrs. Hall had counted on, she couldn't get out of the yard.

A little later, Mrs. Hall glanced out the window to see how her little girl was doing. She didn't see her. So she went outside to find Martha Layne. She looked in every corner of the yard. It was useless. Martha Layne was nowhere to be found. Mrs. Hall's heart stood still.

Trying to sound calm, she called: "Martha Layne...?" No answer.

"Where are you, Martha Layne?" Still, no answer.

Just then, she noticed the front gate. Was

it unlatched? "That can't be," she thought. "I checked it myself when I brought Martha Layne out to play. I know it was closed and the latch was hooked."

Mrs. Hall couldn't imagine where she was. Then she wondered. Is it possible that Martha Layne could have unhooked the gate after all? It was hard enough for an adult. Surely her three-year-old hadn't figured it out!

But she had.

Now Mrs. Hall had only one thought. She had to find her daughter. Fortunately, the area outside their yard was a large, open field. There were no deep holes or uncovered wells that a small child could fall into. But, there was one HUGE danger. It laid just beyond the field—the open highway. Cars drove very fast on it. If Martha Layne wandered into this road, she could easily be run over.

In a panic, Mrs. Hall ran down the dirt path to the main road. Frantically, she looked in first one direction and then the other. There was no sign of Martha Layne. Mrs. Hall took some comfort in knowing that, at the least, Martha Layne hadn't been run over. But by now, Mrs. Hall was so worried and upset that her legs could barely hold her up. "Where could Martha Layne be? She *has* to be here—somewhere."

"The grocery store," she thought. "Maybe someone at the grocery store has seen her." It was just across the highway. She rushed across the road and hurriedly threw open the door. Then, she stopped dead in her tracks. There sat Martha Layne on Miss Frances's lap—having a grand old time.

Martha Layne could see by the look on her mother's face that she had done something wrong—something *very, very wrong*. Miss Frances saw it, too.

"Now, Mama—don't spank her!" she pleaded with Mrs. Hall. "She didn't get on the road. I saw her and brought her across." Smiling at Martha Layne, she said, "We were having just the nicest visit while we waited for you—weren't we, Martha Layne?"

Not daring to take her eyes from her mother's angry face, Martha Layne nodded "uh-huh."

Martha Layne didn't get a spanking. The truth is, Mrs. Hall didn't much believe in spanking or yelling at children. Back then, many parents punished their children this way. But, she thought there were better ways to teach children to follow rules and do what they were told. Sometimes she sent Martha Layne to her room to think about what she had done. Other times, they had a "little talk."

The talks usually took place in her special little chair. This time, they didn't have a little talk. They had a *BIG* talk about how she was *NEVER EVER* to open the gate again, and she was *NEVER EVER* to leave the yard without permission.

All good leaders are curious and want to go exploring. And all good leaders figure out ways to do things that others think are impossible. Martha Layne had to learn that good leaders don't do dangerous things that can hurt themselves or others. They try to make things as safe as possible for everyone.

Chapter 4

Scared but Hanging In

Growing up in the small town of Bagdad probably helped Martha Layne learn more about how to be a good governor than anything else she did. Very few people lived there. They all knew each other and looked after one another. That meant Martha Layne had lots of good neighbors and friends. They showed her how to do things that children in big cities didn't often get to do. But some of the things scared her a little.

One such time was when Martha Layne went home with Sally after church. Her parents realized she had a curious nature and needed to find safe ways to use it. The visits with Sally opened a whole new world of adventures for her. Sally lived on a farm.

Martha Layne liked everything about Sally's farm—riding on the tractor and hay wagon, helping take food to the men working in the fields, playing in the piles of straw—everything. But what fascinated her most were the animals.

The first thing she always wanted to do when she got to Sally's house, was go to the barn. She had to see the cows and their new babies. But before she could go to the barn, there was lunch and a nap. Martha Layne didn't really like taking a nap. Sally explained that farm work was hard. Martha Layne wouldn't be much help if she was hungry and tired.

The problem was, Martha Layne was usually too excited to go to sleep at naptime. So, Sally read to her. Martha Layne loved story time and tried to stay awake. But when they read in the front porch swing, she always fell asleep. The gentle swaying and the quiet, lazy creak of the chains moving back and forth made her so drowsy she couldn't keep her eyes open.

Once the nap was over, Martha Layne was ready to head to the barn. More than anything, she wanted to help feed the baby calves. She thought they drank from bottles, just like babies do. After all, they are baby cows. But Sally didn't use a bottle. She brought out a metal bucket. Sticking out from the side of it was a long rubber tube called a nipple. It looked kind of like a giant white thumb.

Sally explained, "The milk goes in the bucket. Then the calf sucks on this nipple—here on the side—and the milk comes out into the calf's mouth."

All of this was new to Martha Layne. She watched quietly as Sally filled the bucket with white, foamy liquid. Soon Sally announced, "Now we're ready!"

Calves may be babies, but they were much bigger than Martha Layne was. Sally warned, "You're going to have to be *very* careful, Martha Layne. Or you could get squashed." To keep Martha Layne safe, Sally lifted her up and set her in a wooden feed trough. The rambunctious calves couldn't reach her there.

To keep the calves from jumping around so much, Sally put one end of a rope around their necks and then tied the other end to a board in the stall. Now it was safe for Martha Layne to help feed them.

Martha Layne felt a surge of excitement standing in front of the calves. They were always hungry. Giving them food was one of the most important things she could do. But, Martha Layne couldn't lift the bucket by herself. Sally had to help. Together, they held it high enough for the calf to reach the nipple.

But, no matter how steady they held the bucket, the nipple kept coming out of the calf's mouth. Trying to get the nipple back, wet noses crashed into the side of the bucket.

"Wham!" went the calf's knobby head.

"Ker-thunk," groaned the bucket.

The racket and sloshing of milk made Martha Layne flinch and jump back a little. Shaken, she knew that whatever "squashing" was, this calf was about to do it to her.

Sally watched the commotion and wondered what Martha Layne would do. Would she cry and

want to go back to the safety of the trough? No, she didn't. She just put her hands back on the bucket and looked the calf straight in the eyes. "Stop it!" She scolded. "You're being bad!"

"Now, Martha Layne, the calf isn't being bad." Sally explained. "It's just too little to know how to drink from a nipple. We have to teach it. Here, I'll show you how."

Martha Layne watched as Sally dipped her finger into the milk. Once it was coated with milk, she took it out and stuck it in the baby calf's mouth. "Once she tastes the milk on my finger," Sally told Martha Layne, "she will want more." The next thing Sally did was drip milk onto the nipple. And, just as she had done with her finger, she gently pushed the nipple into the calf's mouth.

It worked! In no time, the calf sucked the nipple just as Sally said it would. Now the calf could have all the milk she needed.

Of course, Martha Layne had to let the calf suck her finger, too. Just like Sally, she dipped her finger in the milk. Squinting her eyes and drawing her shoulders up under her ears as if to brace herself, she timidly offered her finger to the calf's eager mouth. What a surprise! The calf's tongue felt rough and scratchy. It wasn't smooth like hers. The sucking didn't hurt exactly. It was more like a tickle. She couldn't help but giggle.

Feeding the calves took lots of courage because they were scary. But Martha Layne believed they needed her so much that she didn't let her fear stop her. She stayed on the job and let Sally teach her what to do, and that's what good leaders do.

Chapter 5

There *Has to Be* a Way

Martha Layne was about three years old when her family moved next door to the Whitmans. Here she found a new interest—chickens. The Whitmans had a little pen of baby chicks right in their front yard.

The first time Martha Layne and Mrs. Hall went to visit their new neighbors, Mrs. Whitman was feeding the chicks. Martha Layne watched as she reached into an old battered bucket, and one handful at a time, scattered ground corn on the floor of the pen. Martha Layne was fascinated by the little yellow feathery fluffs as they scurried around, scratching and pecking the food.

"Tap—tap—tappity—tap—tap—tap." Then they would stop and look up to see if anyone was watching them. "Tappity—tap—tappity—tap."

When Mrs. Whitman saw how much Martha Layne enjoyed the chickens, she gave her a handful of corn and let her feed them, too. From that time on, Martha Layne just *had* to help feed the chickens.

Once again Martha Layne was a good little helper. She always took her small sand bucket with her. It was just what she needed to hold the corn.

Everything went well, except Martha Layne could not always get to the chickens. A giant fence stood between her yard and the Whitman's yard. The only way to get around the fence was for her mother to walk her up the big highway that ran in front of their houses. Most of the time, Mrs. Hall was too busy to take her. Martha Layne had learned a long time ago *NEVER EVER* to go on the highway without a grown-up. She was stuck!

One day Martha Layne stood with her bucket in her hand, looking through the fence. She just knew that the chickens were hungry and needed her to feed them. "There *has to be* a way," she told herself.

All at once, she saw the answer! There was a tiny space between the two wooden posts at the end of the fence. It was just big enough for a small child her size to squeeze through.

Excited by her discovery, Martha Layne ran to the house to get her mother. It was just as she said. By scrunching between the posts, she could get to the Whitman's house without going out on the forbidden road.

Anxiously, she watched her mother's face. Finally, Mrs. Hall said, "All right. You may go between the posts to see the chickens—as long as Mrs. Whitman doesn't mind."

Martha Layne knew Mrs. Whitman wouldn't mind. "She needs me to help her," Martha Layne said.

And Martha Layne was right.

Good governors believe if people are hurting in some way, there has to be a way to help them. If they don't have food to eat, there has to be a way to feed them. If they are sick and need a doctor, there has to be a way for them to see one. If a pet is stuck in a tree, there has to be a way to get it down. But just like Martha Layne learned, it is important to find ways to help that don't break the rules.

Chapter 6

Looking Ahead

One thing all good governors do is look ahead to see what might be needed in the future. For example, in some places it always snows in the winter. So in those places, salt is stored up to sprinkle on the roads and snowplows stand ready when the snow comes. Good governors know that diseases like measles and chickenpox make children very sick, so they make sure there are enough vaccines to protect every child. They know that children and pets living in the city will always need a safe place to play and exercise, so they save land for playgrounds and parks.

The first time Martha Layne tried to plan ahead was when she was only four years old. It started when she saw her daddy do a very strange thing. He stuck a long stick with four spikes on it into the ground. He called it a pitchfork. It helped him pitch dirt and grass out of the way to make room to plant seeds deep in the ground. This time he didn't use the pitchfork in the garden.

Sitting beside him was an empty coffee can. There was dirt in it. After each turn of the pitchfork, he bent down and picked up a clump of dirt. He broke it apart in his hands and sifted it through his fingers. It was like he was looking for a buried treasure.

Then Mr. Hall grinned. "Ahhh—now we're getting somewhere. A nice big, fat, juicy one. The fish will *love* you!" Dangling from his fingers was a long, wiggly, red worm.

This was the first time Martha Layne had heard about fishing, so she didn't really understand why her daddy needed worms. But that didn't matter. If he needed them, she would help him find them. Before long, she was watch-

ing for worms like they were the most important things in the world.

Some worms weren't easy to catch. They stuck their heads out of a hole in the clump of dirt. When she reached for them, they slithered back down into the hole. She had to be extra careful with those only halfway out of the hole. If she pulled too hard, they broke in half. The best ones were those that slid out on top of the dirt and seemed to be just waiting for her to pick them up.

As was her habit, Mrs. Hall checked on Martha Layne to see how she was doing. She knew she was with her father and set out to find them. When Martha Layne saw her coming, she yelled, "Look Mother, I'm catching worms!" Proudly, she held one up for her to see. Mrs. Hall wasn't the least bit impressed.

"Oh, Martha Layne—look at you! You're all dirty." Martha Layne hadn't even noticed. Her work was much too important to worry about a little dirt.

Mr. Hall laughed. "Come on, Mama," he teased. "You can help, too."

"Not me," she muttered and turned back toward the house. "You couldn't pay me to touch those slimy things."

The next week, a boy named Thomas came to dig the garden for Mr. Hall. Of course, Martha Layne was right there watching him work. Suddenly, without a word, she ran to the house as fast as her short little legs could carry her.

Thomas didn't know what had happened. He was afraid something had scared her. But before long, she was back carrying her bucket.

"Wait, Thomas, wait," she called out to him. Now he was totally bumfuzzled. "What's the matter?" he asked. "What's wrong?"

"Look!" she exclaimed. "It's a worm! My daddy needs this worm. I have to catch it for him."

Poor Thomas. He could hardly dig the garden for Martha Layne stopping him every time she saw a worm. "I'll never get through," he sighed.

But he did.

And her daddy? Well, Martha Layne had planned for the future. The next time Mr. Hall wanted to go fishing, the worms he needed were right there, ready and waiting for him.

Chapter 7

The Helper Needs Help

When Martha Layne was five years old, her family moved to a place where there were even more things to see and do. Her new neighbors, Mr. and Mrs. Cox, had chickens, but they also had hogs, baby pigs, and a big horse named "Ol' Nell."

The Coxes were very nice people. They told Martha Layne she could visit their animals any time she wanted. Best of all, she could get there without going on the road.

One afternoon when Martha Layne went to check on the animals, the Coxes weren't home. So, she made her rounds alone. Ol' Nell was her first stop. Ol' Nell looked hungry, so Martha Layne decided to give her some corn.

Mr. Cox kept his corn in a special building called a corncrib. Martha Layne knew what to do. She had been there with him many times. But she didn't like the way the corncrib smelled. Boards were missing from some of the walls and the rickety floor jiggled and creaked every time anyone walked on it.

When Martha Layne got to the corncrib, the mama sows and baby pigs were in the pen beside it.

Now, animals may not know everything humans know, but most of them have some idea about when they're going to get fed. When the hogs saw Martha Layne, it was around the time Mr. Cox fed them. They thought she was going to feed them. So they started squealing with excitement, shoving and pushing each other to reach her.

But, Martha Layne had no plans to feed them. Mr. Cox told her they were dangerous and could hurt her. "You let me feed the hogs," he warned the first time she helped him. "They're too rough for you. Go over there and feed Ol' Nell. She wouldn't hurt a fly."

Since it was safe to feed Ol' Nell, Martha Layne continued her journey. She pushed up the wooden handle on the corncrib, opened the door, and went inside. Somehow the room was darker than she remembered when she was there with Mr. Cox. And she didn't remember the noisy, impatient hogs being right outside the corncrib. The more they thought she was going to feed them, the louder their grunting and snorting became.

Martha Layne decided she wouldn't stay long. Working quickly now, she grabbed two ears of corn for Ol' Nell from the huge yellow pile that filled half the room.

Suddenly the door swung shut. Now it was *really* dark in there. Time to leave, she told herself. But when she pushed on the door, it didn't open. She pushed again—really hard this time. The door didn't budge. It was no use. The latch had dropped down on the outside of the door. To her horror, she was trapped.

She tried to be brave, but it was hard. The

hogs were digging into the cracks in the wall of the corncrib with their hungry snouts—trying their best to get in. She could feel their hot breath. It was getting harder and harder to breathe. Worst of all, they were banging and pushing against the flimsy wall. She was sure it was going to break down any minute—and they were going to get her. Finally, she did what any kid would do. She yelled and yelled and yelled.

"Mother! Come quick! Help me! Mother! Help!"

Mrs. Hall was in the kitchen talking with Grandmother Hall when she heard the cries for help. Martha Layne had never sounded like this before. She had to be in big trouble. Alarmed, Mrs. Hall raced out the door without even stopping to lay down her dish towel.

"I'm coming, honey! Hold on, Mother's coming!"

Grandmother Hall hadn't heard Martha Layne so she didn't know what had happened. But she knew it was something big. She got to the window just in time to see Mrs. Hall running straight towards the bushes. "What

is Mary doing?" Grandmother Hall wondered with alarm. "She's going to hurt herself!"

But when Mrs. Hall got to the bushes, it was like she had magic wings. Even with a dress on, she flew over those hedges like they weren't even there. All she could think of was Martha Layne being trampled to death by either Ol' Nell or the hogs. If she was going to save her, she couldn't waste any time.

When she reached the barnyard, Martha Layne wasn't with any of the animals. "Where are you, honey? Tell Mother where you are!"

"Here—over here!" quivered the familiar little voice. But the hogs were making so much noise Mrs. Hall couldn't hear her. She looked everywhere. Finally, she turned in the direction of the corncrib. Thinking she saw something move, she moved closer to it. That's when she spotted four tiny fingers wiggling desperately at her through a crack between the boards.

This time Martha Layne didn't get a little talk from her mother. Mrs. Hall knew Martha Layne was just trying to be helpful. The only thing that upset Mrs. Hall was being scared half to death. But she figured Martha Layne was just as scared and had learned a good lesson on her own.

The adventure in the corncrib didn't stop Martha Layne from taking risks when she thought she was doing something helpful. But it taught her a very important lesson. Some jobs are too big and too dangerous to do by yourself. Even the bravest leaders can't make important things happen unless they have help.

Chapter 8

Understanding Changes

One day Mr. Hall said, "Come on, Martha Layne. Let's go on an adventure. Let's go see something."

"Something" was a litter of seven puppies. Martha Layne laughed at the way they lost their balance and tripped over each other. Then Mr. Hall surprised her.

"Pick out a puppy and we'll take it home with us." He barely got the words out of his mouth before she swooped down and wrapped her arms around the little brown and white frisky one. She buried her face in his fur and cuddled him. Mr. Hall laughed. There was no way he could

change his mind now. The family had just gotten a new member—Spanky.

Soon, Spanky and Martha Layne were the best of friends. They went practically everywhere together. When she went outside, he went outside. When she went inside, he went inside. When she took a nap, he took a nap. They were buddies. She began to think of him as kind of like a little brother or sister.

One day Martha Layne went inside to get her bucket. Spanky waited outside because he knew she was getting ready to feed the chickens. It was one of his favorite things to do. He was so excited about going to the Whitmans that he started running circles in the yard. Each trip around the circle was faster and faster. The circles got bigger and bigger. And the bigger they got, the closer he got to the forbidden highway.

Before he knew it, he was out in the road. Then, a very sad thing happened. Spanky got hurt. He had darted into the road so fast there was no way the car could stop in time.

Martha Layne heard the wheels squeal and Spanky yelp. She ran outside. A man was running toward the road. It was Tom, a neighbor who lived a few houses away.

"Spanky!" she yelled as she ran to him. When she got there, he was lying on the pavement, bleeding.

Tom reached Spanky first. Carefully, he picked him up and carried him to his little owner. At first he didn't know how badly Spanky was hurt.

Martha Layne was crying. "Is Spanky going to be all right?" she asked him.

"Martha Layne," Tom said gently. "Spanky is hurt. I'm going to take him home with me where I can take care of him. But I'll bring him back when he feels better." She was very upset, but glad that Tom was going to help her injured puppy.

Each day, Martha Layne asked about Spanky. "Is Spanky well yet? Is he coming home soon?" Finally, her parents told her he wasn't ever going to be able to come home. "Spanky died," they said. "He was hurt so bad that the veterinarian couldn't make him well."

Martha Layne tried to understand. "He broke the rule, didn't he? He got on the road."

"Yes," her parents told her. "And a car hit him." Then they reminded her, "That's why we don't want you going on the road by yourself."

In time, Martha Layne was able to talk about Spanky without crying. But she never stopped missing her little friend. Her father could see that she was lonely.

"Do you miss Spanky?" he asked. Martha Layne nodded her head. "Well, Spanky can't come back," he said, "but, if you want, we can get you another puppy."

She hadn't thought about getting a new puppy. She had only been thinking about Spanky. "Could we?" she asked.

"I don't see why not," he said.

The next day, Martha Layne had a new friend. She named him Fuzzy. And just like Spanky, he did everything she did. But this time, Martha Layne made sure he learned the rule about the road. She was *not* going to let Fuzzy get hurt like Spanky did.

It was when Spanky died that Martha Layne learned things don't stay the same. They change—sometimes for good reasons and sometimes for sad reasons. She still remembered Spanky and missed him. But now she had Fuzzy. She didn't have to be sad and lonely anymore.

Good governors know they can't stop sad things from happening—sometimes even when people follow the rules. But they find ways to help people make things better—just like good parents do.

Chapter 9

Making Things Better

What a good governor wants more than anything is to make life better for people. When Martha Layne was about five, she found a way to make "Mr. Le-lon's" life better. His name was really Mr. Leon, but Martha Layne never quite said it correctly.

Mr. Leon lived three houses away from Martha Layne. He was a quiet man around seventy years old. Everyone liked him. She knew him because he walked by himself a lot. He loved nature and liked being outside—just like she did.

Mr. Leon had the habit of meeting some men in the little town each day at a certain time.

They sat on a special bench at the store and talked for a while.

Martha Layne was outside one morning when Mr. Leon went by. "Hi, Mr. Le-lon," she called out cheerfully. Surprised, Mr. Leon looked in her direction to see who had spoken to him.

When he spotted Martha Layne's grinning face, he smiled. "Hulloo," he said. She knew he lived by himself and figured he must be lonely, like she was before Fuzzy came to live with her. The funny thing was, when Mr. Leon smiled at her, he didn't look lonely anymore. That gave her an idea. If she smiled and said "hi" to Mr. Leon every day, she could make him happy. From that day on, Mr. Leon was a very important person in her life.

Fuzzy was always at Martha Layne's side, so he said hello to Mr. Leon, too. Each morning they ate their breakfast and then hurried out to the end of the sidewalk. Sitting side by side, they waited for him.

Sometimes she overslept. "Oh no," she would cry running to the door. "Mr. Le-lon—I've missed Mr. Le-lon. I have to see him."

Mrs. Hall would stop her. "Come on, Martha Layne," she insisted. "Let's put on your shoes and eat your breakfast first.

"Oh Mother, I can't," she pleaded. "I just *have* to say 'hi' to Mr. Le-lon. Please!"

Mrs. Hall never understood why seeing Mr. Leon meant so much to Martha Layne. "Why does she think she has to be out there *every* morning?" she wondered. To her, it was just plain foolishness.

What she didn't know was Martha Layne believed Mr. Leon *needed* to see her each morning. She would be letting him down if she didn't smile, wave, and say hello to him every day. The urgency in her daughter's pleas made it very difficult for Mrs. Hall to say "no" to her.

"All right, Martha Layne, go on—but hurry up!" she needlessly called after her.

Most of the time Martha Layne hadn't missed Mr. Leon.

"Hi, Mr. Le-lon."

"Hullooo, Martha Layne."

He always kept walking. Every once in a while he asked, "How are you?" It never mattered to Martha Layne that he didn't talk to her. She just wanted to see him smile and to make him happy.

Their task done, Martha Layne and Fuzzy would walk back to the house. They always had a look of great contentment on their faces—like they had just done something very important.

And they had.

They made Mr. Leon's life better.

That's what good leaders and governors do. They go to the people and talk to them. They listen to them. They let them know they are important. This may be the most important thing good leaders do.

Chapter 10

The Hard Worker

To become the first woman governor of Kentucky, Martha Layne had to work very hard. But that was not a problem, for she was always a hard worker. Most of the time, she wouldn't even stop to rest until the work was finished. There was one time though, when she wished she had.

It happened when she helped her daddy plow the garden with Ol' Nell. Mr. Cox let him borrow her for the day. Mr. Hall hitched the wooden plow to the horse's leather harness. Then, he set Martha Layne on Ol' Nell's back. "Hold on tight with your legs or you'll fall off," he cautioned.

Ol' Nell could only see straight in front of her because she had black patches or blinders on each side of her eyes. Farmers used them to keep horses from being scared or surprised by a squirrel or something running across their path. Since Ol' Nell couldn't see to turn, it was Martha Layne's job to make sure they went in the right direction.

Riding Ol' Nell was great fun—at first. But after an hour or so, Martha Layne's legs began to hurt. She had been sitting still for so long that her legs started aching. She tried to move them but lost her balance and almost fell off of Ol' Nell.

"I've got to hold on tight," Martha Layne thought. But the tighter she gripped her little legs, the more they throbbed. There was only one way to stop them from hurting. She would have to get off of Ol' Nell and walk around. But, Martha Layne couldn't do that. Her daddy wasn't finished yet. She couldn't stop until he and Ol' Nell did.

Now, you might ask, what would be wrong with Martha Layne getting off of Ol' Nell and resting her legs for a little bit? The answer is, nothing would be wrong with it. But in Martha Layne's young mind, she had an important job to do and she was going to see it through—no matter how much her legs hurt.

After what seemed like a very long time, the plowing was finally finished and her father stopped for the day. When he lifted Martha Layne off of Ol' Nell, she was relieved and happy. But when her feet touched the ground, her legs were so sore and stiff she could barely move. She even wondered if she would be able to walk to the house. Of course, she was able to walk to the house, but it wasn't easy.

That night Martha Layne's parents noticed that she didn't play much. They were even more surprised when she went to bed early.

The next morning they watched as she slowly hobbled down the stairs. Every step was slow and painful. Finally reaching the bottom, she sat down and rubbed her sore, aching legs. Mrs. Hall felt sorry for her. Sounding as miserable as she looked, Martha Layne asked her, "Mother, do you reckon Ol' Nell feels this bad, too?"

Mrs. Hall smiled. "Ol' Nell worked hard too, didn't she, honey? But no—I don't think she feels bad. I'm sure she feels just fine."

And she did.

Good leaders always care about their workers. Martha Layne showed this when she wondered how Ol' Nell felt. But it would have been good if Martha Layne also thought about her own poor legs. Good leaders understand the importance of breaks and rests. They take care of their workers AND themselves.

Chapter 11

"I Can Do That!"

When it was time for Martha Layne to start school, she was eager to go. She dreamed of many new adventures in that big brick building. There would be many new things to learn, and a lot of people to see.

One day her teacher said, "Children, something very special is about to happen. Your parents are coming to visit our classroom."

At this news, the children became so excited they all started talking at the same time.

"But children," she continued, "our room must look as pretty as it can. I think we need some flowers. Do any of you have flowers you could bring?" The first hand to go up was Martha Layne's. Her teacher smiled approvingly and said, "Thank you, Martha Layne."

When Martha Layne got home and told her mother that she needed flowers to take to her classroom, there was a problem. "Martha Layne," she said, "we don't have even one flower in our whole yard. Where will I get any flowers for you to take to school?"

Martha Layne wasn't sure. People didn't buy flowers back then unless it was a very special occasion like a wedding. But her class needed flowers and Martha Layne just *had* to help. She knew her mother was good at figuring out how to do hard things. Martha Layne knew her mother would think of something.

And she did.

Thanks to their neighbor, Miss Abbey, and others that lived nearby, Martha Layne found all the flowers her class needed. All she had to do was tell her neighbors why she needed them and they were happy to help her.

Another day the teacher said, "Boys and girls, we're going to take a field trip and we need some parents to drive their cars." Again, Martha Layne's hand was the first in the air.

Just like with the flowers, when she got home, there was a problem. Again, her mother was astonished. "Martha Layne, you know I don't have the car. Your father takes it to work every morning. How am I supposed to drive you and your classmates on a field trip?"

A really good thing about the people in Bagdad was the way they shared what they had with each other. If children needed a ride to church, someone would pick them up and bring them home when it was over. Or if they needed a ride to a ballgame, a neighbor would take them. So, it was not unusual for parents who had cars to help with field trips. Mrs. Hall just didn't have a car to drive.

Now it may seem wrong that Martha Layne kept volunteering her mother for activities at school without asking her. She didn't mean any harm. She just wanted to help her teacher. That made her a little too eager to say "yes."

It's also important to remember that Martha Layne had confidence that her mother could find a way to do almost anything. All she had to do was get her mother to see how important the project was.

Good governors know the importance of helping—even when, at first, people don't think they can. They know that almost everyone loves to help and feels good when they do. They also know that everyone can help in some way—even if it seems small. Mrs. Hall didn't have the flowers she needed, but she gave Martha Layne the idea of where she might find them. That was very helpful.

Chapter 12

The Leader

Martha Layne acted as a leader each time she talked her parents into helping her. The first time she persuaded her friends to go along with one of her ideas, was when she was nine years old.

It happened on a hot summer day. Martha Layne and four of her friends sat under a shade tree wishing they could go swimming. But Bagdad didn't have a swimming pool; there wasn't even one in the bigger town of Shelbyville. The closest one was more than twenty miles away. And, with her father taking their one car to work every morning, her mother had no way to drive them to the pool.

"Think about how nice it would be—jumping in, splashing each other," dreamed Martha Layne's friend Mary Elizabeth.

"I wouldn't even hold my nose," bragged Martha Layne's three-year-old cousin, Cindy.

Martha Layne was listening to their talk when she had an idea. "Hey! Why don't we build our own swimming pool?"

"Our own swimming pool?" they chorused.

"Yes! We can do it! It might take a little while, but we can do it," she assured them.

"But where?" Shirley wanted to know.

"How?" asked Patsy.

Martha Layne had it all figured out. They would build the pool in her backyard. There was plenty of room behind the garden. All they had to do was dig a big hole. "If we all dig, it won't take us very long," she continued. "But I don't have enough shovels for everyone. Can you find something at your house to dig with?"

By this time, all of her friends were excited. "Yeah!" they shouted and ran off toward their homes.

Martha Layne found a shovel and hoe in the

shed where her father kept his tools. Keeping the shovel for herself, she gave the hoe to Cindy.

The truth is, Cindy was too young to help but she was so proud to be with her cousin "Marf" that Martha Layne didn't have the heart to hurt her feelings by leaving her out.

"Come on," she called to Cindy. "While they're gone, we'll decide where to build the swimming pool." It had to be a big space to hold all the people in Bagdad.

"Okay, Marf," said her little shadow with an air of importance.

Soon the others were back with their digging tools. Martha Layne led them to the spot she had chosen. They plunged into their work with great enthusiasm—digging and chopping and chopping and digging. Unfortunately, the ground was very dry. It was so hard that when the girls chopped at the dirt, the handles of the hoes stung their arms.

Suddenly, Patsy yelled, "Hey, look out! You almost conked me on the head!" Looking sorry, Cindy apologized and promised to be more careful.

After what seemed like hours, a small hole began to form in the ground. "It won't be long now," Martha Layne announced to her little crew. "Just think, we'll have our very own swimming pool—right here! Everyone in Bagdad can use it. And it won't cost them any money, either."

Just then, her mother came out.

"Hi, girls," she said. "What are you doing?"

"Marf and us are building a swimming pool," Cindy bragged proudly.

"Oh—I see," said Mrs. Hall. "Well, are you really sure you want to build a swimming pool? They are a lot of trouble, you know."

"Oh yes. We're sure," said Mary Elizabeth. "And Martha Layne said we could come swimming *anytime* we want."

"That's fine," she said. "But how are you going to keep the water clean? It will keep getting dirty and you'll spend all of your time trying to get it clean. You don't want to swim in old muddy water, do you?"

The little helpers looked at Martha Layne. They wanted her to tell Mrs. Hall that the water wouldn't get dirty.

"Tell her, Marf. Tell her we can do it," said Cindy, tugging at her idol.

But Martha Layne was quietly thinking it over. She had been sure they could dig a big hole. She had just forgotten all about the water. "There's no way to get the water clean?" she asked her mother.

"No," came the discouraging reply. "You would have to dip the water out with a bucket and even then, you couldn't get rid of all the dirt."

Martha Layne saw that her mother was right. She hated to say the words, but she had to. "I guess we can't do it."

Her friends couldn't believe what they were hearing. They studied her face to see if there was any chance she would change her mind. Her sad look said it all. The answer was "no."

Disappointed, they picked up their tools and walked away. Their heads were down but Martha Layne could still hear the voice of a loyal follower: "We could've had our very own swimming pool if Mrs. Hall hadn't stopped us!"

The fading voices agreed. "Yeah, if Mrs. Hall hadn't come out…!"

Martha Layne had made a mistake. But like all good leaders, she learned something important from it. If she had shared her idea with her mother, she would have learned about the problems before they started digging. From that time on, Martha Layne would find out everything she could about a project before she decided to tackle it—especially if she was going to ask others to help her.

Part II
...Who Grew Up...

Chapter 13

Martha Layne Collins

When Martha Layne was thirteen years old, her family moved to Shelbyville. Shelbyville was a much bigger town than Bagdad. There would be many new things to do and lots of new people to meet. This should have made her very happy. But it didn't.

Martha Layne loved living in Bagdad. She couldn't imagine moving somewhere else, especially to a big new town. All of her friends were in Bagdad. Leaving them made her very sad. But, whether she could imagine it or not, her family moved. The worst part was that some of the kids in her new school made fun of her because she came from a small town. They said she was "country" and called her a "hick."

Martha Layne worked very hard to make new friends. At first, it didn't work. She was treated like an outsider—like she didn't belong in their class. When picking leaders, her classmates always skipped over her and picked someone else. It was very disappointing because Martha Layne liked being a leader.

Mrs. Hall could see that Martha Layne's feelings were hurt. But she encouraged her not to be upset. There would be plenty of other jobs she could do. "Do the jobs you are given," she coached her, "and later you'll get your chance to do the bigger things you want to do."

Martha Layne always liked being a part of everything going on around her. She also liked working with others, so Mrs. Hall's advice was easy to follow. Before long, she found that a lot of the kids were actually very nice. Only one or two were unfriendly.

Just as Mrs. Hall had said, Martha Layne got to do many special things. She was chosen to be a cheerleader for the basketball team. She was in several clubs. One was the 4-H club where all the members had to work on a project. Martha Layne chose to raise and show a calf named Sunshine. Sunshine lived with her aunt and uncle on their farm in Bagdad. Martha Layne loved to visit them. She practically lived there in the summers.

"Showing" Sunshine meant that she was in contests with other calves. The contests were often held on local fairgrounds. For Sunshine to have any chance of winning a show, she had to look really good. She had to have a bath. Not a bathtub bath. A bucket bath with warm soapy water. Martha Layne dipped a brush into the bucket and scrubbed Sunshine all over. The soap was washed off by spraying water on her from a garden hose. Next, Martha Layne shined Sunshine's hooves and painted them with black shoe polish. And then there was the tail. Martha Layne braided it. Later, she unraveled the braid and combed it. Sunshine now had wavy ringlets to show off.

All spruced up, Sunshine was ready to go. When their time came, Martha Layne placed a leather halter over Sunshine's head and led her into the show ring. Each calf was paraded around the ring and a judge picked the winner. Sometimes a cow or calf got tired and laid down in the dirt. It was always embarrassing to the owner. Fortunately, Sunshine never laid down in the ring. She was a good calf, but she never got first prize. Martha Layne didn't mind. She just loved being a part of the excitement.

During her high school years, Martha Layne's parents were quite active in the election of government leaders. They worked at campaign headquarters putting letters in envelopes and stamping them to mail. Sometimes they went to the doors of people's houses to hand out information.

Of course, Martha Layne was right there with them.

By the time Martha Layne finished high school, she had many opportunities to be a leader. She was in so many clubs and activities that her parents wondered where she found the energy to do everything. One of the best things she did was help start a youth center for teenagers.

Then came college. In the 1950s and 1960s, girls in college mostly studied to become either a secretary, nurse, or teacher. Martha Layne decided to become a teacher of home economics. One of the interesting things about studying home economics was getting to learn about new inventions. Part of her classwork was to teach others about new inventions. That meant she had to study radio and television. She did so well that she was given her own radio show.

After college, Martha Layne married Bill Collins. Her name changed from Martha Layne Hall to Martha Layne Collins. She began teaching school while he studied dentistry and became Dr. Bill. They began their family with their first child, Steve. Three years later, Marla was born. Just like his mother, Steve always liked meeting people. Marla especially loved animals. Instead of a calf like Martha Layne had, Marla had a horse named Coe.

Martha Layne was glad that Steve and Marla liked going to school and were good students. But some of the children in their community struggled with school work. Martha Layne worried about them. She knew everyone needs a good education. So each summer, any students who wanted extra help could come to her home and she helped them.

From childhood on, Martha Layne looked for ways to help people. When she saw them struggling, she found ways to help. Martha Layne was always willing to share her gifts and talents with others. Not all people are like that, but good leaders are.

Chapter 14

The Politician

Martha Layne's parents started teaching her about the importance of sharing with others when she was very young. As she grew older, she watched adults share with each other. Mr. Cox shared Ol' Nell, parents drove their cars to take children on field trips, and neighbors shared their flowers.

When someone didn't want to share, she often heard the word "fair" spoken. "That's not fair! Mama gave it to me—not you!" Or, "It's only fair that I get to choose first because it's my ball." Some people always seemed to be willing to share. Others wanted to keep things for themselves.

The next thing Martha Layne learned was there are two kinds of sharing. One kind is "personal" sharing. This kind of sharing says, "I don't have to share with you because it is mine. I own it. I get to decide." It's true. The person doesn't have to share. It's fair to say "no." It's just not being very friendly.

Family sharing is another kind of personal sharing. Fairness is especially important when only one member of the family can use something at a time. During these times, fairness means taking turns. "It's my turn to sit in the front seat!" Or, "I get to play on the iPad. You've had it for hours and hours!"

Parents work hard to be fair. They want their children to know they love all of them the same. It's really upsetting when those they love argue, so they set rules for fairness. Then, when the arguments start, they just say: "Now, what are the rules?"

The other kind of sharing is "public sharing." That means all the people get to use something for free. For example, everyone gets to use public roads, public schools, public health departments, and public parks. They are called public because the people pay for them through taxes.

Sharing is sometimes hard, even when people know and like each other. But, public sharing is especially hard because most people don't know each other. Fairness is very important.

In families, parents set the rules for fairness. For the public, the government sets *laws* to try and make sure everything is fair for everyone. Anyone using something paid for by the public must obey these laws.

The *government* is a system of people working together to make rules and laws about how to live well together. The people working in the government to make these laws are called *politicians. Voters* select the politicians to represent the communities where they live.

Take public roads and highways as an example. Everyone can travel on them, but drivers must obey laws like those telling them how fast they can drive. Even those riding bicycles and walking have safety rules they must follow.

One of our best public safety laws has to do

with obeying the stoplight signal. It was invented in 1923 by a man from Cleveland, Ohio named Garrett Morgan. Mr. Morgan was out driving one day when he came upon an accident. It happened at a crossroad—the place where two roads come together and cross over each other. Two cars had reached a crossroad at the same exact time. Neither driver knew who was supposed to stop. So, neither one did. They ended up smashing into each other.

Mr. Morgan was deeply troubled by what he saw. He knew this accident could happen to other drivers. Then, he had an idea. A signal could be used to tell drivers when to go and when to stop. He invented the stoplight. It uses three colors—yellow, red, and green. Yellow tells people to slow down when the light is about to turn red. The red light means stop and stay stopped until the color changes to green. Green signals that it is safe to cross through the intersection or crossroad. Mr. Morgan's stoplight is still used today—almost one hundred years later. It has prevented many accidents and has saved hundreds of lives.

Politicians heard about the stoplight and

made speeches in their communities about how it could help everyone be safer when crossing a road. The people liked the new invention and told the politicians to vote for it. It became law when more politicians voted for it than against it. The law said government money would pay for stoplights to be put up all across the United States. It also said that everyone must obey the signals.

When Martha Layne was in college, she learned about inventions and told people about them. But she wasn't a politician. She didn't work for the government. Still, Martha Layne knew about politicians. She liked the way they could help so many people all at one time.

One day a politician named Wendell Ford asked Martha Layne to help him in his campaign to become governor of Kentucky. He said he wanted to work with all of the politicians in Kentucky to bring new ideas and inventions to communities. She decided to help him.

Martha Layne liked working in Mr. Ford's campaign. She used everything she had learned from her radio program and making speeches.

She did such a fine job that other politicians began asking her to help them, too. Soon there was so much work to do that she had to stop teaching at school.

It wasn't long before people began asking Martha Layne to become a politician herself. She liked the idea. But there was a big problem. In the 1970s, people weren't used to voting for women. Nearly all of the politicians were men.

She decided to try and ran for the Clerk of the Kentucky Court of Appeals. She had always liked the way the courts cared about fairness. As Clerk of Courts, she could carry out laws that helped people be fair to each other. She especially liked the way courts settle arguments about who's right and who's wrong.

Running for a political office was a new adventure for Martha Layne. The first thing she had to do was tell the voters which *political party* she belonged to. Was she a member of the *Republican* party or the *Democratic* party? Both parties are very important. Each has a different but special job to do. That's why good government needs for the two parties to work well together.

The Democratic party has the important job of making sure the government never stops making changes that make life better for the people. It might be protecting the environment with solar powered cars, or finding a way to give health insurance to everyone. People who like new changes listen a lot to Democrat leaders.

The Republican Party has the important job of making sure government doesn't change too much, too fast. They ask a lot of questions about whether an idea will work or not. They want to know how much it will cost. Is it really needed?

Is it too risky and unsafe? Anyone asking these kinds of questions usually wants to hear what Republican leaders are saying.

When Martha Layne had the idea to build the swimming pool, she thought like Democrats do. It was for everyone. It would make people's lives better. She thought, "Let's do it!" But when Mrs. Hall came out, she did what Republican leaders do. She asked Martha Layne and her friends if they were sure they wanted to dig a pool. How were they were going to clean the dirty water?

Mrs. Hall pointed out everything that could go wrong. She asked questions that needed to be asked. While Martha Layne's idea for change was a good one, she and her friends just didn't have what they needed to make it work. Mrs. Hall helped her see this.

Martha Layne was always full of ideas for changing things, so she chose to be a Democrat. Her first task was to become the person nominated by the Democratic Party. That meant she had to run in a *primary election* against the other Democrats who wanted the job. The same was true for the Republicans. The winner of each party's primary election would then run against each other in a *general election.*

Other candidates besides the Democrat and Republican run in the general election. Independent candidates don't belong to any political party. There are also candidates from other smaller parties, such as the Green Party. They just don't have primary elections.

Once the parties pick their candidate in the spring primary election, the November general election campaign begins.

Many people encouraged Martha Layne not to be disappointed if she didn't win her first contest. She could always run again in another year if she lost.

But they needn't have worried. Martha Layne won more votes than any other Democrat in the primary election. Then, she won more votes than any candidate in the general election.

Martha Layne was now the Clerk of Courts. She was on a new adventure as a politician. She could use politics to help lots of people.

Martha Layne liked being a politician, but

her new job only lasted for four years. If she wanted to keep on being a politician, she had to run for a different government job.

She decided to run for *lieutenant governor* of Kentucky. The most important work of a lieutenant governor is to take over as leader of Kentucky when the governor travels outside of the state or becomes too ill to do the job.

Campaigning for lieutenant governor was hard work. But this time, Martha Layne knew the people were willing to vote for a woman. They already had a woman lieutenant governor. Her name was Thelma Stovall and the people liked what she did for them.

Martha Layne began each campaign day for lieutenant governor at 6:30 in the morning. She traveled to all of the different towns and cities of Kentucky— talking to people and listening to what they needed. She heard about leaky roofs in school buildings. Others mentioned roads so full of holes and ruts that they were unsafe to drive on.

The days were long and tiring for all those who campaigned with her. But just like when she rode Ol' Nell, Martha Layne never stopped. Every town held voters. She asked everyone she met to vote for her—even the guy putting gas in her car.

As it turned out, it was a very good thing that she worked so hard. The primary race against the other Democrats was very close. But Martha Layne won.

Then she was back on the road again campaigning for the general election. This time, the votes were even closer. But, once again, Martha Layne won!

Now, she was Lieutenant Governor Martha Layne Collins.

In her new job, Martha Layne continued getting up early in the morning. She traveled to all 120 counties of Kentucky to see the people. She listened for new ideas about ways to make their lives better. She made lots of speeches to people of all ages.

Most interesting of all, Martha Layne was governor for 500 days during the four years she was lieutenant governor. Every time the governor left the state, Martha Layne was in charge and became the governor. Each time the governor came home to Kentucky, she returned to her duties as lieutenant governor again. That is a whole year and ten months. She learned everything she could from every one of her experiences. Then, her four years as lieutenant governor were almost over.

Now, the people began to talk to her about taking on an even bigger job for them.

Part III
...To Be Governor

Chapter 15

Governor of Kentucky

The people saw that Martha Layne was a good politician. She had come to their towns and schools to find out what they needed. She talked to veterans of the military. She went into coal mines to learn what life was like working in the deep, dark, underground caves. She visited older people in nursing homes. And she showed concern for the many people who told her they needed a job.

The people felt they knew her. They could see that she wanted to help them and trusted her as their friend. So they asked her to run for a job no woman had ever done in Kentucky before. They wanted her to be their next governor.

Once again, Martha Layne wondered if a woman could win. She had learned a lot as lieutenant governor. And she had lots of ideas for new ways to help Kentucky. So, she decided to try.

Women were especially excited to help her campaign. They stuffed letters in envelopes and went door-to-door, handing out information about her to their friends and neighbors.

By this time, she knew all about campaigning. And on the first Tuesday of November 1983, Martha Layne Collins was elected the fifty-sixth governor of Kentucky. Kentucky's first woman governor—ever!

People all across the United States took notice. The election of a woman to govern a state was very rare. In the history of the country, only six women before her had served as governors. Four were elected after their husbands could no longer serve. The other two won the seat the same way Martha Layne did. During the first two years of her term, she was the only woman governor in the entire United States. Each of the other 49 governors were men.

Kentuckians knew that what they did was a very big deal. That election night in November brought hundreds of helpers and friends together in a big ballroom in Lexington. With fingers crossed and hopeful hearts, they waited for hours to find out who won. Then, it became official. Martha Layne Collins was the next governor of Kentucky. Cheers went up all around the room. People hugged each other and jumped up and down. Some even cried with happiness.

One thing candidates always do on election night is speak to their crowd—even if they lose. With her victory assured, Martha Layne stepped up to the microphone. Joy filled the room. She looked around at all the happy people. Their hard work had mattered. Now they were basking in their reward.

Yes, Kentucky had made history. But the real magic of the moment belonged to the girls and women. Martha Layne felt the magic, too. The first four words she spoke were: "How sweet it is!" A second round of deafening cheering and whistling went up. The crowd loved her!

The official day of celebration was December 13, 1983. The day began with a church service in her hometown of Bagdad. Imagine her delight as she passed by her elementary school and saw all of the children and teachers gathered on the lawn to wave and smile as she went by.

After her time in Bagdad, she traveled back to the State Capitol in Frankfort for the rest of the celebration. When she arrived, a long parade of colorful bands and beautiful floats awaited her. People lined the streets for miles to show their new governor they were proud of her and believed in her.

All of the excitement reminded her of a day years earlier when President Truman pulled into Shelbyville on a train. The people waited with great anticipation for his arrival that day. Now, they were waiting for her. But, she wasn't arriving on a train. The new governor rode on a handsome carriage drawn by four beautiful Canadian horses. Prancing and tossing their regal heads, they seemed to command: *"Look at us! We're strong. We're magnificent!"*

But the attention of the crowd wasn't on them. All eyes were straining to be the first to catch a glimpse of the slender woman waving and smiling from atop that beautiful old carriage.

Along the route, two twelve-year-old boys sat perched on the limb of a maple tree. As the carriage drew near, one was heard to say, "It'll be different. It'll be nice."

Thinking it over, his friend replied, "It will give everyone a chance to see which will be better—a boy or a girl."

Martha Layne was thinking about that, too. She knew people were going to watch her closely. But today, she was celebrating a wonderful day with women and girls everywhere.

Shortly after the coach and horses reached the capitol, the inauguration ceremony began. Martha Layne placed her hand on three Bibles held by Steve and Marla, who were now college students.

"I, Martha Layne Collins, do solemnly swear that I will support the Constitution of the United States and the Constitution of Kentucky, will administer justice without respect to persons, and will faithfully and impartially discharge and perform all of the duties incumbent upon me as governor according to the best of my ability..."

These words were a promise from Martha Layne to do everything she could to be a good leader. And just as she had done many years ago in her little chair, she promised not to break the rules.

Then Governor Martha Layne Collins made a speech to the thousands of people gathered in front of her. She must have been thinking about Miss Frances, Sally, and all her cousins and friends in Bagdad and Shelbyville when she told everyone: *"I will always remember from whom I come, and with whom I remain."* She wanted them to know she would never forget everything they did for her.

The day ended with a grand ball held in the State Capitol Rotunda. Everyone dressed up in their finest clothes. Dr. Bill escorted the new governor down the long, white marble staircase to join the people. Everyone could tell by the determined look on her face that she couldn't wait for her new adventure to start.

It was all glorious. Now, she could help lots of people—all at one time.

This time, she had a plan with lots and lots of good people to help.

Chapter 16

Keeping Her Promise

Governor Collins and her family moved into the beautiful mansion that the people of Kentucky provided for them. She invited thousands of people to come and see her there. Not only did Dr. Bill, Steve, and Marla live there, but so did their dogs—Jinx and Riley—and their cat, Peppy.

But Riley didn't stay very long. He missed being outside and running around anytime he wanted to. Everyone could see he was unhappy. They decided to let him live with some friends on a farm.

Governor Collins had a fine, hard-working staff. Her office was the biggest one she had ever had. And so was her desk. She read and signed lots of important papers on that big desk.

She traveled out to see the people and made many speeches. Sometimes she flew in a helicopter named Sikorsky.

She helped children by making sure they had more money for their schools. She also created new adventures for them, like the Bluegrass Special Olympics, the Governor's Scholastic Cup, and the Governor's School for the Arts.

She often visited these events to cheer the children on in their new adventures. When they saw her, many ran to her—waving their arms, yelling, "Governor! Governor!" She always made sure that before she left, she spoke to each one of them, no matter how long it took.

To keep her promise of helping people find new work, she met with business people and industries. They agreed to bring more jobs to Kentucky than anyone ever thought possible for such a small state. Some say her biggest accomplishment was convincing the Toyota company to build its cars in Kentucky.

She visited countries like England, Japan, Korea, China, and Saudi Arabia, where she made many new friends for Kentucky.

The President of the United States, Ronald Reagan, invited her to the White House in Washington, D.C. In 1986, she traveled to England and had lunch with Queen Elizabeth at Buckingham Palace.

It was all very, very exciting.

Kentucky was proud of the history they made with their first woman governor. And, best of all, the boy in the maple tree got the chance to see that "girl" governors "rock." That's why more and more women every year are being elected governors of their states.

In the 1980s, Kentucky governors were only allowed to serve for four years. Now they can hold office for eight years. When Governor Collins's term was over, she turned her attention back to education. She always loved sharing the things she learned with young people. For six years, she was president of St. Catharine College. Later, she worked at Georgetown College and the University of Kentucky. Murray State University in western Kentucky named their Center for Industry and Technology in her honor. And now, in the town of Shelbyville where she graduated from high school, a beautiful new school has been named Martha Layne Collins High School.

And just think, it all started with a courageous, adventurous little girl who loved people, and more than anything else, just *had* to help.

Part IV
Words from Governor Collins

Chapter 17

Keepers

When you go fishing and catch a fish, you get all excited. And, so does everyone around you—even strangers. "I got one, I got one!" you yell. The others cheer you on, sometimes warning you not to let your fish get away. When it's finally landed and flopping at your feet, someone usually says, "Wow! That's a keeper!" Or, "Sorry, it's too small. We have to throw it back." We can use this idea in other areas of our lives, too. When something is judged to be a "keeper," it means that it's too good to forget or throw away.

The stories in this book were my mother's "keepers." Of all the many things I did while

growing up, these memories and stories were the ones she chose to remember and to pass along to others. Even though I was no more special than other children, some things I did were special to her.

That's the way it is with all parents. Every child creates keeper stories. Right now, you are doing things that your parents and grandparents will always remember. Someday they will tell their keeper stories about you to your children. What will these stories be?

Many of these stories will be about the things you did that surprised those who took care of you or made them laugh. Maybe you did something that was supposed to be too hard for you to do. Or, you did something especially nice without anyone telling you to do it. Perhaps you played "pretend" and were a teacher or you engineered a city with your LEGO® blocks. Whatever the stories are, those who have watched you grow up might end up saying: "That's why I always knew what you would do when you grew up."

Some of my mother's keeper stories were about my getting into trouble. These were good stories because she could tell I was just trying to be helpful. That's why I was glad for her little talks with me. That way I always knew what I had done wrong. And, I learned what to do differently the next time.

One of the most important things I had to learn was what I could do by myself and what I needed help to do. Maybe it was because I was an only child, but I did a lot of things by myself. Some of those things really scared my mother. Have you noticed that older people get the most upset with you when you do something that scares them? That's because they believe the most important job they have is to keep you safe.

Never be afraid to ask for help. When you are a child, most any adult can teach you the things you want to know. I had my parents, Sally, Mr. Cox, Mrs. Whitman, and many others to help me along the way. When I went to school, I had even more teachers.

You have many teachers around you, too. Let them help you. Let them teach you the things they know. Grandparents make especially good teachers. I know, because I'm a grandparent. I have always loved helping my grandchildren.

My five grandchildren, Taylor, Catherine, Alex, Will, and Ellie are all grown up now. Each one is special in their own way. When we all get together, Taylor and Catherine sometimes hear stories about their father, Steve. Alex, Will, and Ellie hear stories about what their mother,

Marla, was like when she was growing up. They are good stories because they are keeper stories.

Try it out for yourself. Turn to someone who loves you and say, "Tell a keeper story about me. Tell me a good one." This will help you remember how special you are. And that's important.

As we end our time together and say goodbye, I want to leave you with the words I say to all of my young friends:

Dream dreams, work hard, study hard, and you can grow up to be anything you want to be.

But always remember—whatever that is—be the best you that you can be.

Martha Layne Collins
Governor of Kentucky
1983–1987

Teaching and Learning Guides

for Educators and Parents

Are you an elementary school educator who would like to learn more about how to use this book in your classroom?

Are you a parent who would like to have some discussion questions to use with your young reader as you read this book together?

If you answered yes to either of these questions, check out the teaching and learning guides for *The Little Girl Who Grew Up to Be Governor: Leadership Lessons and Stories From the Life of Martha Layne Collins,* Second Edition by Frances Smith Strickland, Ph.D.

Available Fall 2021 on the website for the book at **www.kidsareleaders.org**.

Appendix

Table A

Female Governors Elected In Their Own Right

Name *Party–State*	Dates served
Ella Grasso *Democrat – Connecticut*	1975–1980
Dixy Lee Ray *Democrat – Washington*	1977–1981
★ **Martha Layne Collins** *Democrat – Kentucky*	1984–1987
Madeleine Kunin *Democrat – Vermont*	1985–1991
Kay Orr *Republican – Nebraska*	1987–1991

Name *Party–State*	Dates served
Joan Finney *Democrat – Kansas*	1991–1995
Ann Richards *Democrat – Texas*	1991–1995
Barbara Roberts *Democrat – Oregon*	1991–1995
Christine Todd Whitman *Republican – New Jersey*	1994–2001
Jeanne Shaheen *Democrat – New Hampshire*	1997–2003
Judy Martz *Republican – Montana*	2001–2005
Ruth Ann Minner *Democrat – Delaware*	2001–2009
Jennifer M. Granholm *Democrat – Michigan*	2003–2011
Linda Lingle *Republican – Hawaii*	2003–2021

Name *Party–State*	Dates served
Janet Napolitano *Democrat – Arizona*	2003–2009
Kathleen Sebelius *Democrat –Kansas*	2003–2009
Kathleen Blanco *Democrat – Louisiana*	2004–2008
Christine Gregoire *Democrat – Washington*	2005–2013
Sarah Palin *Republican – Alaska*	2006–2009
Beverly Perdue *Democrat – North Carolina*	2009–2013
Mary Fallin *Republican – Oklahoma*	2011–2019
Nikki Haley *Republican – South Carolina*	2011–2017
Susana Martinez *Republican – New Mexico*	2011–2019

Name *Party–State*	Dates served
Maggie Hassan *Democrat – New Hampshire*	2013–2017
Gina Ramaindo *Democrat – Rhode Island*	2015–2021
Michelle Lujan Grisham *Democrat – New Mexico*	2019–Present*
Gretchen Whitmer *Democrat – Michigan*	2019–Present*
Janet Mills *Democrat – Maine*	2019–Present*
Kristi Noem *Republican – South Dakota*	2019–Present*
Laura Kelly *Democrat – Kansas*	2019–Present*

* at the time of publication, June 2021

Table B

Female Governors Under Special Circumstances

Name (Party–State) *Special Circumstances*	Dates served
Nellie Tayloe Ross (D–WY) *Replaced deceased husband*	1925–1927
Miriam "Ma" Ferguson (D–TX) *Surrogate for husband*	1933–1935
Lurleen Wallace (D–AL) *Surrogate for husband*	1967–1968
Vesta Roy (R–NH) *Moved up from State Senate*	1982–1983
Rose Mofford (D–AZ) *Moved up from Sec. of State*	1988–1991

Name (Party–State) *Special Circumstances*	Dates served
Jane Dee Hull (R–AZ) *Moved up from Sec. of State*	1997–2003
Nancy Hollister (R–OH) *Moved up from Lt. Gov.–12 days*	1998–1999
Jane Swift (R–MA) *Moved up from Lt. Gov.*	2001–2003
Olene Walker (R–UT) *Moved up from Lt. Gov.*	2003–2005
M. Jodi Rell (R–CT) *Moved up from Lt. Gov.*	2004–2011
Jan Brewer (R–AZ) *Moved up from Sec. of State*	2009–2015
Kate Brown (D–OR) *Moved up from Sec. of State*	2015–Present*
Kay Ivey (R–AL) *Moved up from Lt. Gov.*	2017–Present*
Kim Reynolds (R–IA) *Moved up from Lt. Gov.*	2017–Present*

* at the time of publication, June 2021

About the Author

Frances Smith Strickland is an educational psychologist who believes that the clues to a meaningful life and fulfilling work are found in early childhood traits. Although her professional energies early on were focused on helping children thrive in public schools, she became increasingly interested in leadership and good leaders as her career progressed. Her interests in education and the need for good leaders converged when Dr. Smith Strickland took special note of Kentucky's first woman governor in 1983. As the state's new leader, Governor Martha Layne Collins made improving public education a major priority for her administration.

Shortly after Governor Collins's term ended, Dr. Smith Strickland married and moved to Ohio. Reflecting back on the things she most admired about her home state, first and foremost was the election of Governor Collins. Dr. Smith Strickland decided to provide a legacy for the children of Kentucky by writing and publishing a book about a woman who accomplished something almost unthinkable in 1983—especially in a small, rural state like Kentucky.

Dr. Smith Strickland had a big task in mind when she began the first edition. She wanted to help children understand how ordinary people accomplish great achievements. To do this, Dr. Smith Strickland drew on the works of John W. Gardner and Howard Gardner. John Gardner was an educator and highly accomplished political leader who wrote extensively about leadership and the traits of good leaders. Howard Gardner's creative work as a developmental psychologist added the dimension of natural intelligences and how they show up in children. With the vivid stories about Governor Collins's childhood adventures provided by her mother,

Mary Hall, *The Little Girl Who Grew Up to Be Governor* began to take shape.

During the thirty years since the first edition, Dr. Smith Strickland's husband, Ted Strickland, was elected to the U.S. Congress and, after twelve years, became the 68th governor of Ohio. As First Lady of Ohio, Dr. Smith Strickland focused her energy on strengthening children and families and continued her commitment to education by initiating the Governor's Institute on Creativity and Innovation in Public Education.

Now retired, Dr. Smith Strickland lives in Columbus, Ohio. With the second edition of *The Little Girl Who Grew Up to Be Governor*, she wanted to extend its reach by drawing on the work and influence of leadership experts Peter Block and Margaret J. Wheatley. While the revision continues to stress the early traits that predict strong leadership skills, it also brings a modern look to issues that affect kids today. Dr. Smith Strickland allows her readers not only to follow a child's emerging leadership skills through story, but also to see how these skills can be used to help others in both big and small ways throughout a lifetime. Along the way, Dr. Smith Strickland wants children to gain an understanding that politics at its best uses the tension found in opposition to create something better and more unifying for everyone.

Born and reared on a farm in Simpsonville, Kentucky, Dr. Smith Strickland received a Bachelor of Science degree in education from Murray State University, a Master's degree in guidance and counseling from the University of Colorado, and a Doctorate in educational psychology from the University of Kentucky. In 1990, Western Psychological Services published her Screening Test for Educational Prerequisite Skills for children entering kindergarten. Currently, she is helping to launch Innovation MotherShip, an initiative designed to help young women recognize and develop their best talents and to use them in ways that strengthen their homes, workplaces, and communities.

Dr. Smith Strickland loves a good conversation. You can contact her through the book website at: www.kidsareleaders.org.

Acknowledgments

There are many people whose work impacts the writing and publishing of a book. In the case of revised versions, this includes past and present people. My greatest fortune has been to have the input and counsel of Governor Martha Layne Collins and her children, Steve Collins and Marla Collins Webb, for both editions. I will always be grateful for their generosity and willingness to help with the additions made to the book.

My publishing team has been incredibly attentive in helping me bring this book to life for the second time. Editor, Heather Doyle Fraser, contributed significantly to modernizing the narrative for young children of today. Much has changed during the last thirty years and thanks to Heather's guidance, I gained a sensitivity that I would have overlooked without her.

I also want to thank Danielle Baird for bringing a fresh eye to the interior and cover design of the second edition. It is almost magical the way she was able to take requests and make them all work. I also want to thank Jesse Sussman for his careful and thorough eye in catching and correcting grammatical details that always make a difference, and for his guidance in the successful launching of the book.

Thanks to the great potential for use by educators, a teaching and learning guide has been developed to accompany the book. Eva O'Mara has been the consummate leader in shaping the work, along with her conscientious team members. Eva, Melissa Sims, Debbie Bernauer, Carolyn Sue Jones, and Angie Smith all volunteered their time, which shows their dedication to helping children learn. I am incredibly grateful to them and also to Jane Wiechel for her part in keeping all of the moving parts going in the right direction. Under her careful eye, all the ships I was responsible for came in on time—all with a steadying hand and gentle sense of humor.

Equally important to me are the wonderful memories that the work on this revision brought back to me. I enjoyed reliving the pleasure I felt listening to Mrs. Hall (Governor Collins's mother) sitting in her chair, a twinkle in her eyes, telling her "keeper" stories. If she was still with us, I'm sure she would have many more stories to tell.

The designer of the original version, Rick Smith, is also no longer with us. I have a great feeling of warmth as I remember Rick (my nephew) and his work on this book. Only twenty-seven years old at the time, I was one of his first clients. Partiality aside, I always felt good about Rick's advice and his selection of Pip Pullen to do the original artwork—which is retained in the revised version. Pip grew up in England and was not familiar with farm life. I still remember the trip we took to Shelbyville so I could show him a corncrib.

I'm also grateful for those from the disciplines of learning, psychology, and leadership whose influence helped shape the direction of this undertaking. John Gardner and Howard Gardner created the underpinnings of the initial publication, which focused on the individual traits of a leader. Judith Worell brought honesty and clarity regarding women in our culture through her in-depth research, writings, and mentoring. And, with this revision, the mentoring of Peter Block and Margaret J. Wheatley is reflected in the expanded perspective of the impact of culture on leadership. Each of the leaders in their field has mattered deeply to me as I've struggled to understand what we must do as a people, both individually and collectively, to ensure healthy systems and nurture thriving communities.

Finally, I want to thank all of the children like Silas, Sylvia, and "Lina," who scrunched in close to a loved one and listened to every word from cover to cover. Their reactions and those of many other adults mattered more than I will ever be able to put into words. All of the many hands that lifted up this effort—young and old alike—have my deepest gratitude.

Frances Smith Strickland, Ph.D.
Author

Teaching and Learning Guides
for Educators and Parents

Are you an elementary school educator who would like to learn more about how to use this book in your classroom?

Are you a parent who would like to have some discussion questions to use with your young reader as you read this book together?

If you answered yes to either of these questions, check out the teaching and learning guides for *The Little Girl Who Grew Up to Be Governor: Leadership Lessons and Stories From the Life of Martha Layne Collins,* Second Edition by Frances Smith Strickland, Ph.D.

Available Fall 2021 on the website for the book at **www.kidsareleaders.org**.

Made in the USA
Monee, IL
26 July 2021